Inky, Snake, and Bee went to the forest. They took Phonic with them on the laptop and set him up in a glade. Then they went off to look for chestnuts.

They liked chestnuts and were going to roast them on a pan in the fire when they got home. They had made a pile of chestnuts next to Phonic.

Snake slithered up the trees and knocked the chestnuts down to Inky and Bee, who cracked the prickly shells and collected the nuts.

One of the chestnuts fell under a tree, and Bee rushed off to fetch it.

"Got you!" said Bee, grabbing the chestnut. She picked it up and stood up. Then, as she looked at the tree, it seemed that the tree looked back at her. "Help!" buzzed Bee in alarm.

Bee fled back to Inky, Phonic, and Snake.

"Help!" she cried again. "That tree was looking at me."

Snake, Inky, and Phonic looked at Bee.

"I think she must have had too much sun," hissed Snake, and shook his head.

"It did," buzzed Bee. "That tree looked at me."

"Do not be silly, Bee," hissed Snake. "Trees cannot look at you."

"Well, this one did," insisted Bee. "Come and see."

Inky picked up Phonic, and Bee led them to the tree.

"There," she said, pointing to it. The tree looked at them and then blinked. "See," whispered Bee. "It *is* looking at us."

"No," said Phonic. "Look, there is a hole in the tree and there is something in the hole."

Snake slithered up and looked inside the hole. He found himself looking at someone who was hanging upside down.

"It looks like a mouse with wings!" called Snake.

"A mouse with wings?" said Inky. "There is no such thing!"

Snake looked into the hole a second time.

"Yup," he said. "It still looks like a mouse with wings to me."

"I think it is you who has had too much sun," said Bee.

"Hmm... a mouse with wings..." mused Phonic. "I think you can see a bat."

“A bat?” said Snake, looking into the hole again. “Yes,” he agreed, “I think it *is* a bat.”

Just then, the bat shot out of his hole and Snake ducked, lost his grip, and fell off the tree.

“Ouch!” yelled Snake as he hit the ground.

The bat hung upside down at the top of the tree, blinking in the sunshine.

"Come back!" Inky shouted up to him. "We will not harm you!"

The bat blinked and then explained, "I was afraid! All the noise woke me up and then, when I looked out, there was a big snake looking in at me."

"Yes, there was," admitted Inky, "but he will not harm you," she added quickly, seeing the bat start to unwrap his wings again.

"Sorry," said Snake. "We were collecting chestnuts. I just looked in to see who was there."

“It is just my family and me,” said the bat. “In winter we sleep in a cave and in summer we live in a big loft. But when we came back this summer, our home was gone. It had been converted into a room.

We have been living in this tree while we look for somewhere else to live.”

"Well," said Phonic, "perhaps we can help. We need to think of somewhere dark that is not too noisy and that has plenty of room for bats to roost in."

"Roast in?" said Bee. "Roast in? Is that a joke, Phonic?"

"No, Bee," Phonic explained. "*Roost* in, not roast in. When bats are hanging upside down and sleeping, it is called roosting."

“What about the shed?” said Bee.

“No, it is too small,” objected Snake.

“There is no room for the bats to hang upside down there,” agreed Inky.

“I think,” said Phonic, “that I have just the spot. Come on, Inky, you will have to help me.”

They set off, Inky carrying Phonic, then Snake, Bee, and the bat. They stopped when they came to the farm.

"There," said Phonic. "What about the big old stone barn? There is plenty of room, it is dark, and there are lots of holes the bats can use for going in and out."

"Perfect!" said the bat, happily. "I must go and tell my family."

"And we can go home and roast our chestnuts," said Bee. "No more trees that blink for me!"